A Little Dachshund's Tale

By April Jean

Illustrations by Kevin Cross

Strategic Book Publishing and Rights Co.

Strategic Book Publishing and Rights Co.
12620 FM 1960, Suite A4-507
Houston, TX 77065
www.sbpra.com

ISBN: 978-1-61897-367-2

For Frances Peabody

Contents

Chapter I: The Little Dachshund

The little dachshund was born on March 23, 2005, in a small New England town. Her first adventure would be her trip from the puppy store. Little did she know that this short trip would be the first of many.

There were a lot of puppies at the pet store that day when she arrived. Many were sad and scared and some, like her, were even sick. The little dachshund had to take medicine to help her feel better, but she was never afraid. She was very brave. One day, while the little dachshund was sitting in the pet store watching the visitors come by, a lady with rings on her toes came in with her mother. She was looking for a puppy. At first, the little dachshund didn't pay her any attention. Lots of people came in to look at puppies, but no one ever picked her. She was tiny and very sick. But then, all of a sudden, much to her surprise, two warm hands reached into the playpen where the little dachshund was sitting. The hands gently wrapped themselves around her tummy

and lifted her up. The little dachshund and the lady were now staring back at each other nose to nose. The lady took the little dachshund to a play area where the two of them sat quietly together and played. The little dachshund tried to play like other puppies, but she was very tiny and very sick. She really couldn't run a lot. She got too tired. She couldn't really wag her tail for very long, because she got too tired, and she never really barked either. The little dachshund did cough a lot though. She was, after all, very sick.

The little dachshund was certain the lady was going to put her back in her playpen and look for another puppy that could run and jump and play more than she could. Then a strange thing happened.

"I think she is perfect," the lady said to her mother.

"She needs a name," the mother said.

"I think she looks like a Frances," said the lady.

The mother giggled. "Okay, but she will need a full name."

"Frances Peabody," answered the lady.

"How did you come up with that name?" the mother asked.

"I don't know. When I looked into her eyes, she just looked like Frances."

Her mother smiled. "Frances Peabody it is then."

Chapter II: Frances Meets Aunty

The little dachshund was so excited that she wanted to jump and bark and wag her tail. She now had a name and would soon have a new home! But really, all she wanted to do was sleep. She was, after all, very sick.

"You can't take that one home," the man said. "She's too sick. You'll have to wait another week or so until she is done with her medicine."

"But I live in New York," said the lady with the rings on her toes. "And I am leaving today."

"Sorry," said the man. "She has to stay here."

The lady gently put the little dachshund back in her playpen. The little dachshund tried to be brave, but she was very sad.

"Don't worry," said the lady, "I will see you again soon."

But the little dachshund didn't believe the lady was ever coming back to the pet store to get her. And she was right . . .

A week passed by. The little dachshund finished her medicine and still no sign of the lady. The little dachshund tried to be brave, but she was now sadder than ever. Then, one morning, she heard the bell sound as the door opened and a woman walked in.

"Hello," said the woman, "my niece from New York came in here a week ago to purchase a little dachshund. I have come to pick her up."

"Yes," said the man, "she told me her aunt would be coming to get her. I'll have her ready in a moment."

The little dachshund was so excited. She would have a new home after all.

"Hello Frances," said the woman. "You'll be staying with Aunty until you are ready to go to New York."

"She's still very sick you know," warned the man.

"I know," replied Aunty, "That's why she will be staying here with me until she is well enough to travel."

Frances really didn't understand any of this. All she knew was that she was going someplace called home with Aunty. Frances liked Aunty immediately. Aunty was warm and smelled good. Aunty held Frances tight in her arms and wrapped her in soft, honeysuckle-scented blankets. Aunty spoke softly and gave lots of kisses. Yes, Frances liked Aunty very much.

Chapter III: The Tall Boy, Uncle, and Ma

Frances stayed with Aunty for nearly two weeks. That felt like a lifetime to the little dachshund. During that time, she met all sorts of people. She met a man named Uncle. He lived with Aunty. Frances loved Uncle's backyard filled with tall, moist, sweet-smelling grass. She also met an older lady that Aunty called Ma. Ma lived down the street from Aunty. Ma cooked all sorts of yummy food for Frances. The smells from Ma's kitchen filled Frances' nose and made her tail wag uncontrollably. Frances loved visiting Ma. Ma gave Frances' velvety ears soft kisses. She held her, cuddled her, and spoke gentle words that lulled Frances to sleep as the smells from Ma's kitchen danced and swirled around her head.

She met a tall boy who lived with Aunty and Uncle. He was home from a place called college. The tall boy liked to play with Frances. She liked him too. He was gentle and let Frances pounce on his tummy. His tummy felt soft beneath her paws and was perfect for pouncing. Frances wasn't sure if the tall boy was *really* falling down whenever she pounced or if he was just playing and simply letting her win. Although Frances was barely three pounds, in her heart she still felt like she could truly tackle the 5'11" boy. She *knew* she could take him. Either way, it was fun to pounce on him.

During her stay with Aunty, Frances was still sick. She still had to take medicine and made several trips to the doctor. But Frances tried not to fuss and was always very brave. Frances, more than anything, wanted to get better. And eventually, she did get better.

Frances was never alone and Aunty took Frances everywhere she went. Frances loved traveling with Aunty. Her favorite way to travel was inside Auntie's bag while swaddled tightly in her honeysuckle blankets. Frances was very happy and knew that she was loved very much. Yet still, she wondered, *Whatever happened to the lady with the rings on her toes who first came into the store?*

Chapter IV: Saying Good-Bye

One day, a woman came into Auntie's house who Frances recognized. It was the lady's mom from the pet store. The woman told Aunty she was getting ready to meet the lady in a place called New York. Soon after, Aunty began packing all of Frances' newly acquired teddy bears, squeaky toys, teething rings, blankets, pillows, vitamins, food, and various treats. For such a little puppy, Frances had a lot of stuff! Aunty and Ma bundled Frances in her honeysuckle blanket and placed her in her favorite traveling bag. Frances knew she was leaving Aunty. Frances, once again, had to be brave.

"Aunty loves you very much," she told Frances as the salty tears gently rolled down her cheeks. "I will see you again soon."

Frances believed Aunty, and although Frances was very sad to be leaving, she was okay because she knew, without a doubt, that she was loved. Frances then nuzzled close to Aunty for one last time. She wanted to make sure she would remember Auntie's warm hugs and sweet honeysuckle smell. The lady's mother then picked up Frances and placed her in the car. Frances slept. On her journey, she dreamt of warm grass, honeysuckle blankets, soft kisses, yummy food, gentle voices, pouncing tummies, and Auntie's arms. She loved napping in Auntie's arms.

Chapter V: Home

When Frances finally awoke, she was in a strange place. The lady was nowhere to be found and Frances did not smell anything familiar. She was very afraid but knew she had to try to be brave. Then suddenly, she heard a familiar voice. She felt warm hands wrapping themselves around her tummy and picking her up. "Hello Frances," whispered the familiar voice. "I told you I would see you again soon."

The warm hands hugged her and the familiar voice continued to whisper softly. It was the lady. Frances was finally in her new home, and for the second time in her life, Frances knew she was loved.

Chapter VI: A Man Named "Honey"

Frances was very happy to see the lady with the rings on her toes. After a long hug, the lady gently placed Frances on the floor. Frances sniffed around and made herself familiar with her new home. The floor was smooth, hard, and a little difficult to move quickly on. Frances kept sliding every time she tried to pick up speed. There were lots of new smells and hiding places to explore. Frances loved to explore. There were also lots of *shoes*. Shoes can be a lot of fun for a puppy. While Frances was enjoying a delicious pair of high-heeled, leather boots, she heard the lady talking to a man. This, however, was a voice that she had never heard before.

"Hi honey, how was your business trip?" the lady greeted him cheerfully.

"This is Frances—the puppy I was telling you about!"

Honey was not impressed. This puzzled Frances, as everyone else she encountered seemed to love her. They always made that same sound too when they first meet her. "Aaawwwwww!" Yet this man the lady called "Honey" did not make this sound. He just sort of grunted and put down some heavy bags in the room with all of the delicious shoes.

Frances decided to work on Honey. She gave him her saddest eyes, sweetest head tilt, and cutest hops on her hind legs. Still, Honey did not make that "Aaaawwww" sound. Frances couldn't believe it! Could Honey actually not like Frances?

This is impossible, thought Frances, *Everyone loves **me**.* And yet, Frances did not get that warm feeling from Honey. This made Frances very sad. She decided to just stick close to the lady and avoid this man called Honey at all costs. This plan worked. For a while . . .

Chapter VII: Bonding

One afternoon, Frances and the lady were at home playing. The man named Honey was at a place called work. Frances liked it when Honey went to work. He was grumpy and didn't make that friendly aaawww sound like the lady did every time Frances rolled over, or simply tilted her head to one side. Frances didn't have to do much for the lady to make that sound. Frances had much more fun with the lady. The lady thought that everything Frances did was cute. Besides all of that, the lady had those rings on her toes that were fun to chase and try to nibble. Frances loved to chase feet.

"You know," said the lady interrupting Frances' attempt to pounce on her feet, "summer is almost over, and I will have to go back to work again soon. We won't have too many more lazy days like these."

Frances became worried. *Who will play with me?* she thought.

"I was thinking of bringing you to work with me though. I bet the children at the school would love you," stated the lady.

Children? Did she say children? Frances understood the word *children*. She liked children. She often met them in the pet store. They gave hugs and had small hands that were perfect for belly rubs. Yes, Frances liked children very much. She wagged her tail to show her approval.

"It's all settled then!" the lady exclaimed with delight. "Come September you will come to work with me every day!"

Frances didn't know who September was, but she didn't care. She was just happy that she wasn't going to be left alone or even worse left with . . .

"Hi honey, you're home early!"

Him! Frances didn't like that man at all.

"I am so glad you are here," the lady told the man. "I need you to watch Frances for a couple of hours."

Oh no! thought Frances.

"I need to run some errands for the school," said the lady.

Frances made a desperate attempt to climb into the lady's

bag so as not to be left behind.

"Why can't you just take her with you like you always do?" asked the man.

"I can work faster if she stays here with you. I won't be long and besides, the two of you need to bond anyway."

Frances didn't like the sound of this "bonding" one bit. The lady placed her on the sofa next to the man. She kissed them both good-bye and said, "I'll be home soon."

Frances and the man were left alone staring at one another, neither of them happy with the situation.

At first, the man just sat there watching TV, not paying much attention at all to Frances except for the occasional stare. After a while, he finally got up from the sofa and placed Frances gently on the floor next to his feet. Frances was grateful to be placed back on the floor, as she was too small to jump down from the sofa on her own. Three-inch legs are not very good for jumping.

"You hungry?" the man asked her.

Frances nearly *did* jump on her three-inch legs! Since she had never actually heard the man speak to her before, the sound of his voice startled her. Frances looked up at the man and tilted her head to one side.

"I'll take that as a yes," said the man.

In the next few moments, Frances was greeted with banging, clanging, scraping, metallic sounds from pots and pans, followed by warm, buttery, salt and pepper garlic smells, which hovered above her in the slightly smoky-scented air.

"Ever have steak before?" the man asked her.

Frances didn't know what steak was, but she knew she was about to find out! Whatever it was, it didn't smell anything like the dry, hard, crunchy, pebble like food the lady always gave her out of a bag. Frances' mouth started to water as the man finished banging and clanging the metal objects and placed the steak and something called a potato on a plate. He then picked Frances up and sat her on his knee as he pulled himself up to a table. Next, he began cutting pieces of steak for himself and even smaller pieces for Frances.

"I hope you like it," the man said softly, handing Frances a bite-sized, buttery morsel. Frances liked it very much. The potato wasn't bad either. By the time she was finished, Frances realized she had never had her belly so full before. It felt good. Frances was now ready for a nap. She curled up next to the man on the sofa as they sat once again in front of the TV. She felt her eyelids getting heavy and they started to droop. Just before she drifted off to sleep, however, she could have sworn she saw the man smiling at her. Nonetheless, Frances had already decided that this "bonding" thing wasn't so bad after all. It was actually delicious. It was even better than high-heeled shoes.

Chapter VIII: Long Walks

After a long nap, Frances finally woke up blinking her eyes and still feeling quite full.

"I suppose I should take you for a walk now," grunted the man.

Frances was suddenly wide-awake, her tail wagging with anticipation. The lady took Frances on lots of walks. Frances mostly traveled in her bag. This walk, however, would be different. The man put on Frances' harness and attached her leash. Frances was surprised that he knew how to put on her harness, as he had never done it before. He did it success-fully and with little difficulty. He then proceeded to carry her down four flights of stairs to the sidewalk.

"Let's go," said the man.

Frances then proceeded boldly at a steady trot with her head held high down Saint Marks Place and across Third Avenue. Along the way, she was stopped dozens of times only to be greeted by an onslaught of "aaawwwws," several pats on the head, and gentle scratches behind the ears. She loved all of the attention though. Frances and the man walked all the way to Union Square and back again. Twelve blocks seemed like a marathon to three-inch legs, but Frances didn't mind. She was having fun. Even the man would break into a jog from time to time, occasionally even smiling while looking down at Frances. Long walks were fun.

From that day forward, it was Honey, not the lady, who took Frances on her long walks every day, except of course when it rained. Frances, after all, hated puddles. Her tummy would get wet. Three-inch legs are not very good at keeping your tummy from dragging through puddles.

Chapter IX: Third Avenue Buffet

Every day Frances would leave the apartment to be greeted by the bustling city streets filled with yummy snacks and smells. She especially enjoyed the buffet of bubble gum along Third Avenue. Every day just as she was about to rip another piece of gum free from the pavement, she would feel a quick tug on her harness followed by the words, "No Frances!" This always puzzled Frances and disappointed her greatly. She was *more* than willing to share her bounty. The long street table was *filled* with sweet, sticky gum and *orange peels!* Oh yes! Lots and lots of orange peels! Frances was great at sniffing out bubble gum and orange peels. She knew, given the opportunity, she could pull up *plenty* of pieces of gum and find more than enough orange peels to fill up at least *three* tummies. Alas, the bubble gum buffet was always a challenge. Although, she was still able to sneak a piece here and there, from time to time, and whenever she did, she was always quite proud of herself.

April Jean

Chapter X: Every Day Is an Adventure

Saturday at 4:30 p.m.-Frances took the lady, and the man she called Honey, out for their daily walk. As usual, Frances took the lead and walked out in front. And as usual, her mind raced steadily as the world passed by:

"Shoes *everywhere* so many shoes! Want to chew."

"Wish we could stop long enough for me to pounce."

"Gotta keep walking."

"More gum up ahead."

"Oops missed another pizza crust; there it goes."

"Gotta keep walking."

"Can't stop; too many feet here."

"Wait! Orange peel up ahead!"

The lady spoke, "How ya doing Frances?"

"Fine! Fine! Missed the orange peel—lady broke my concentration."

"There goes a pigeon."

"Move too fast whenever I get close—could catch it if the lady would just drop the leash."

"Don't wanna *eat* the pigeon . . . just *really* wanna catch it."

"Look, more pizza crust!"

"Not quite sure what that is."

"Smells good though."

"There's that tugging again."

"Gotta keep walking."

"I love walking."

"Wish they wouldn't tug my harness."

"I smell more gum."

"Gotta keep walking."

"I love walking."

"I love steak. I wonder if the man will make steak."

"I love the man."

"I love the lady too."

"There goes a squirrel!"

"Gotta keep going."

"Can't catch it today."

"Maybe tomorrow."

"I'll catch him tomorrow."

"She's gotta drop that leash though."

And so it went on for Frances . . . She was very happy living in the city, and she never forgot her journey along the way to get there. She would take many trips in the future and would even return to New England to visit. She was a happy little dachshund and *every day* for Frances was like an adventure.

The End.

Photo by April Jean

CPSIA information can be obtained at www.ICGtesting.com
Printed in the USA
BVOW010654150113

310560BV00001B/75/P